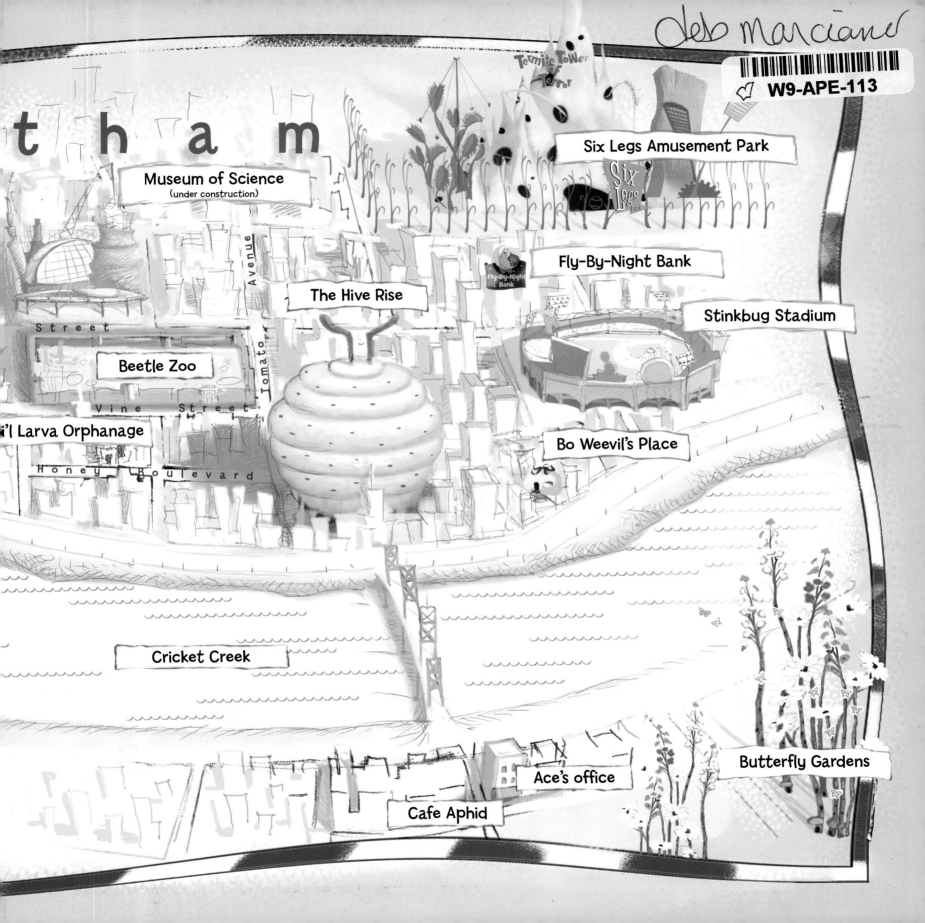

You know it's springtime in Motham City when little bugs are playing in the street, Butterfly Gardens is in full bloom, and our hometown team, the Stinkbugs . . . is in last stinking place.

Welcome To
Butterfly Gardens
If You Lived Here, You'd Be Home by Now

Model
Chrysalises
Now Open
Inquire
Within

Go Stinkbugs! Motham

BUGSY
1

But not this year. A rookie named Bugsy Goldwing had the whole town abuzz.

My gal Xerces and I are big Stinkbug fans. We were counting the days to the play-offs when a gorgeous damselfly fluttered into my office.

Her name was Madame Damselfly. She was a legend in Motham City: a no-nonsense lady with a heart of gold and a wicked curveball. Hundreds of hard-luck little bugs had grown up in her Li'l Larva Orphanage—and more than a few ended up in the Bug Leagues. She'd known Bugsy ever since he was a little stinker.

"Bugsy has a problem, detective," said the damselfly.

Sports
Goldwing
Signs with
Stinkbugs

Owner Pop Fly Says
Bugsy Could Make
Stinkbugs a
"Big Contender"

Sports
THE MOTHAM BUZZ TUESDAY APRIL 7
Stinkbugs Win
First Game

Goldwing Shines

The Big Stink
Up Close with
Stinkbug
Rookie Sensation
Bugsy Goldwing

Sportsbug Illustrated
MVP?
Rookie
Stinkbug
Bugsy
Goldwing

Stinkbugs

Madame Damselfly showed us an old picture.

"Hey, that's Bugsy's lucky bat!" I blurted out. "We saw him swat a huge home run with it against the Chicago Grubs last night."

"It's a genuine, one-of-a-kind, autographed, 'Lou Earwig Big Swat' bat," said Madame. "All my boys wanted it. So I held a home-run contest, and Bugsy won the bat, fair and square. I taught my boys to be good sports, detective, but that bat made them all jealous."

"Bugs will be bugs," said Xerces with a sigh.

"Bugsy got the worst of it. Most of the time, stinkbugs, . . . well, stink. The other bugs teased him. But that didn't bother Bugsy—it made him try harder. He practiced with that bat all the time—even though it was bigger than he was! I always used to tell him: it's not the size of the bat; it's the size of your heart. Bugsy has a big heart."

"So what's the problem?" I asked.

"Last night after the game, someone stole the bat," said the damselfly. "Bugsy called me this morning and asked for my help. That bat's worth a fortune, detective, but it means more than that to Bugsy. He's very superstitious—he thinks he can't hit without it. You've got to find it," she said.

I stepped up to the plate and took the case.

First stop, the new Stinkbug Stadium.

Coach Pee Wee Reeks was tossing batting practice to Bugsy when I arrived. A tragic flypaper accident had squashed Pee Wee's baseball career and left him with a peg leg. But he still had something left on his fastball.

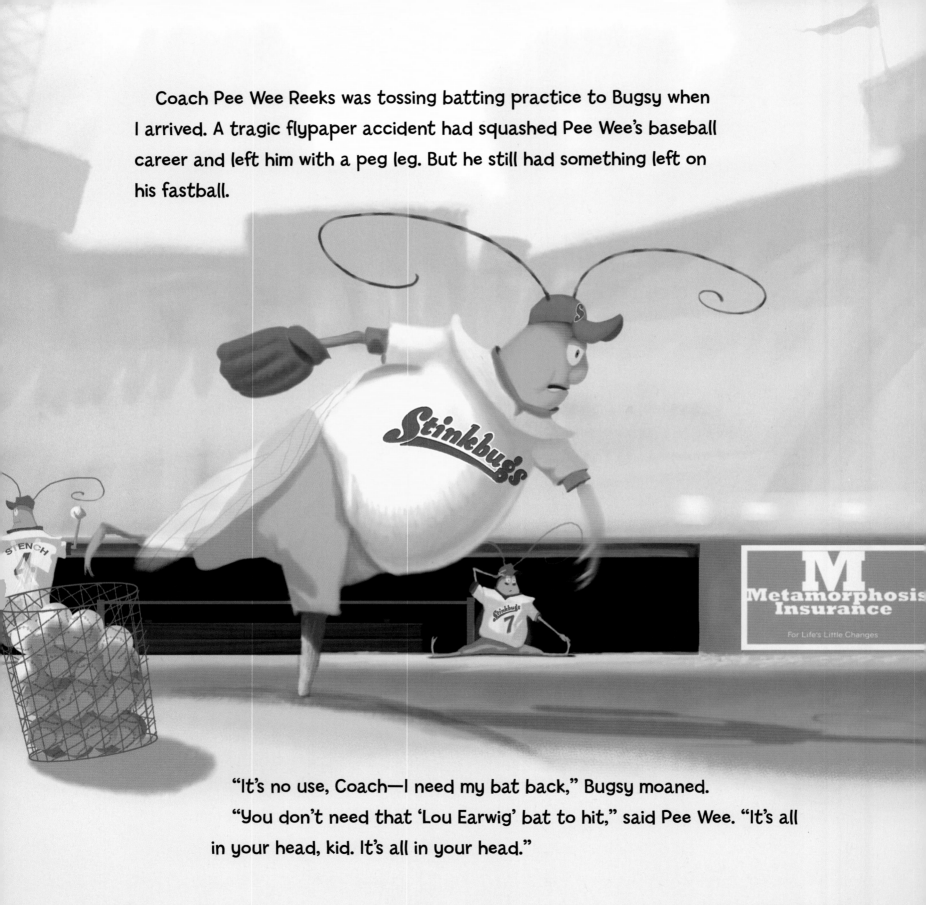

"It's no use, Coach—I need my bat back," Bugsy moaned.

"You don't need that 'Lou Earwig' bat to hit," said Pee Wee. "It's all in your head, kid. It's all in your head."

Bugsy smiled when I mentioned Madame Damselfy. "I love her, detective—she's like a mother to me," he said.

I asked him if he knew who might have taken his bat.

"I don't know," he said. "I put it in my locker after the game last night. Today it was gone. Everyone knows I can't hit without it."

Bugsy sighed and trudged away to join his team.

The Pillbugs rolled over the Stinkbugs 6-0. Bugsy struck out four times. I headed to the locker room afterward to look for clues.

Nothing smells worse than a Stinkbugs locker room after a loss.
The place was empty—but then I heard someone coming.

I could have been a fly on the wall. I settled on being a lacewing in a towel cart.

In the shadows I spotted one of those no-good Roach brothers with a broom. He stopped in front of Bugsy's locker and fingered Bugsy's uniform like he was planning to swipe, not sweep.

"That'd make a nice souvenir for someone," I said.

The roach almost jumped out of his exoskeleton.

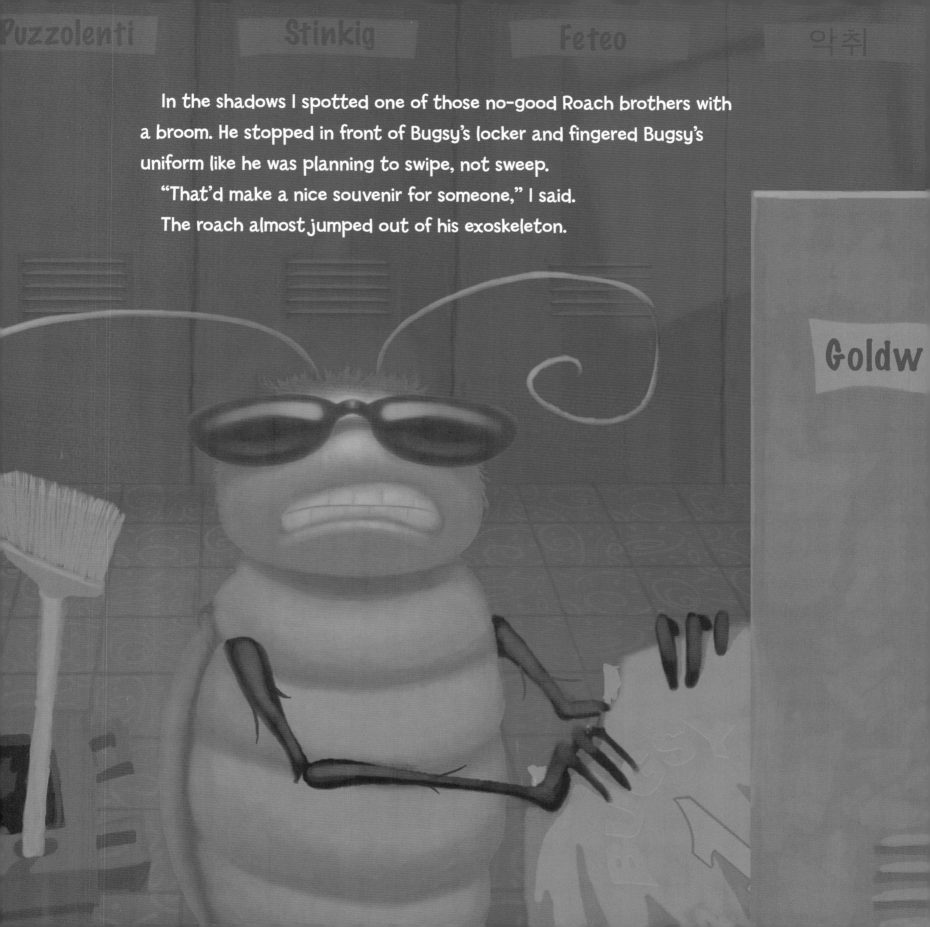

"I wasn't doing nothin'," the roach sputtered.

"Just like you did nothing to his bat?" I asked.

The roach's jaw dropped. "I don't know nothin' about no bat."

"Sure you don't," I said. "So how about I turn on the lights and we talk about it?"

The roach started to sweat. "Oh, that ain't fair, detective. I'm a roach. Lights go on and I have to skedaddle. This place is full of sharp corners. I'll get hurt."

"Too bad." My finger touched the switch.

"OK, I took the bat, all right? Some bug made me a deal: I steal the bat and give it to him, and he slips me some extra cash."

"What bug?" I asked.

"I dunno. It was dark. But he had on a Detroit Tigerfly cap."

"So where's the bat now?" I asked.

"Who knows?" the roach said. "I left it by the recycling bin, like I was told. That's the last I saw of it."

I thought of Madame Damselfly's picture—and the only Tigerfly in it. Then I flicked on the lights and left the room. The roach hit the door with a splat.

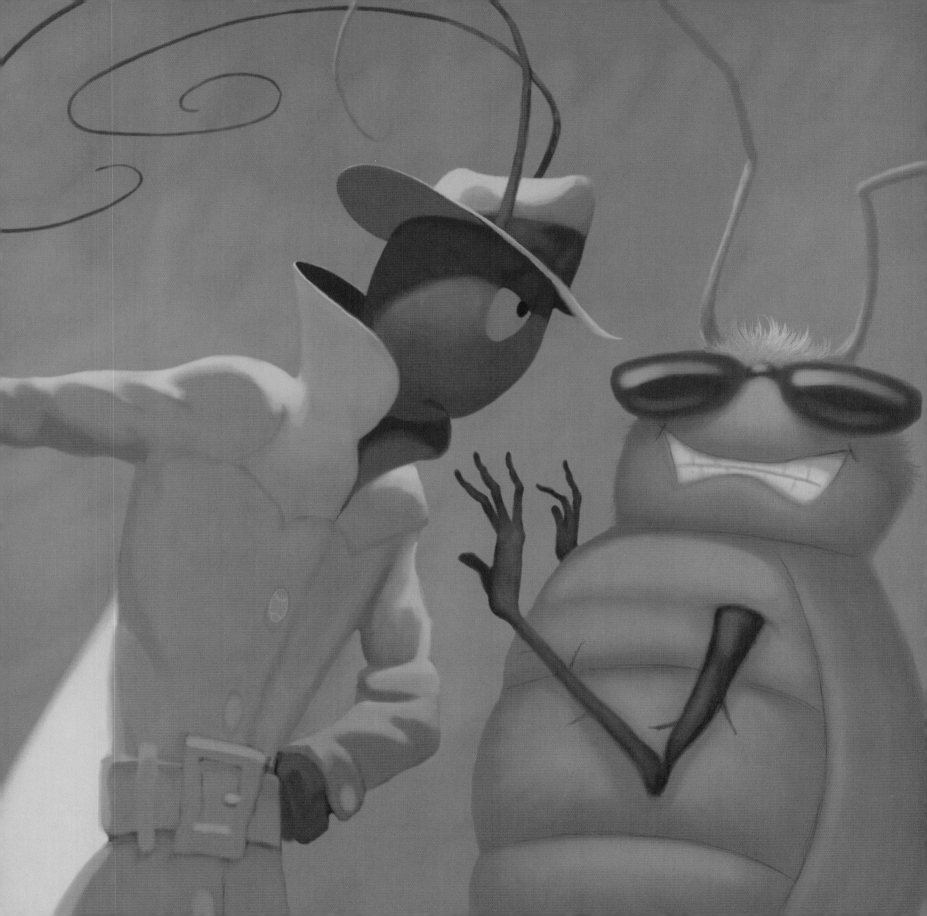

The next day Xerces, my pal Sergeant Zito, and I left Motham City and flew to see the Tigerflys play the Leafhoppers. If the Stinkbugs started stinking again, the Tigerflys were a lock to make the play-offs.

The Tigerflys' star, Fly Cobb, kept his spikes long and his conversations short.

"Bugsy always got teased in the orphanage because he smelled funny," said Fly. "But no one was laughing when he won the bat, detective. We all wanted it."

"Enough to steal it?" I asked.

"Not me, detective. I steal bases, not bats." He winked at Xerces.
She smiled. I glowered.

"Why don't you go ask Hoppi Leafhopper?" Fly continued. "If Bugsy
can't hit, Big Hoppi could win his seventh straight MVP award. Seven's
a big deal to Hoppi."

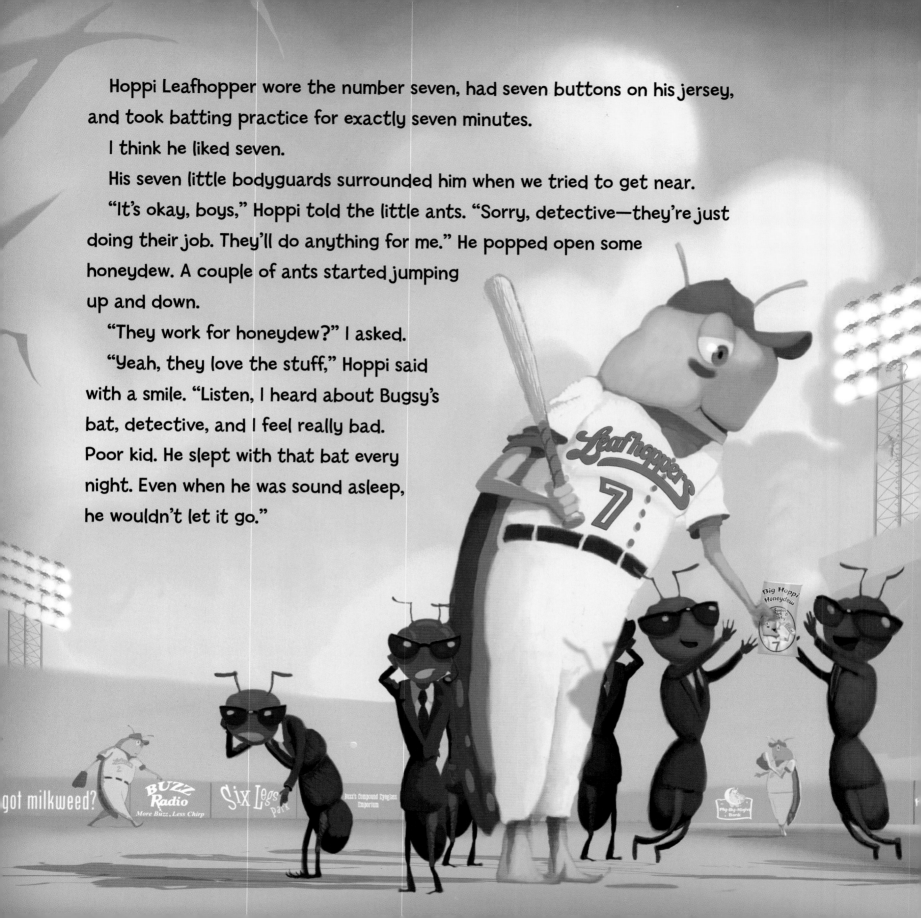

Hoppi Leafhopper wore the number seven, had seven buttons on his jersey, and took batting practice for exactly seven minutes.

I think he liked seven.

His seven little bodyguards surrounded him when we tried to get near.

"It's okay, boys," Hoppi told the little ants. "Sorry, detective—they're just doing their job. They'll do anything for me." He popped open some honeydew. A couple of ants started jumping up and down.

"They work for honeydew?" I asked.

"Yeah, they love the stuff," Hoppi said with a smile. "Listen, I heard about Bugsy's bat, detective, and I feel really bad. Poor kid. He slept with that bat every night. Even when he was sound asleep, he wouldn't let it go."

"How do you know that?" asked Xerces. "Did you try to take it from him?"

Hoppi blinked. Then he smiled again. "If I were you, I'd start with Mickey Mantis," he said. "He never liked Bugsy, and he used to prey on the smaller bugs all the time. But you better hurry. The Mantises are playing at Swamp Stadium tonight, and the last dragonfly leaves in ten minutes," said Hoppi.

We got to Swamp Stadium just in time for the Skeeters-Mantises game. After the game we met with the famous Mickey Mantis. He was a killer ballplayer with a big-league temper.

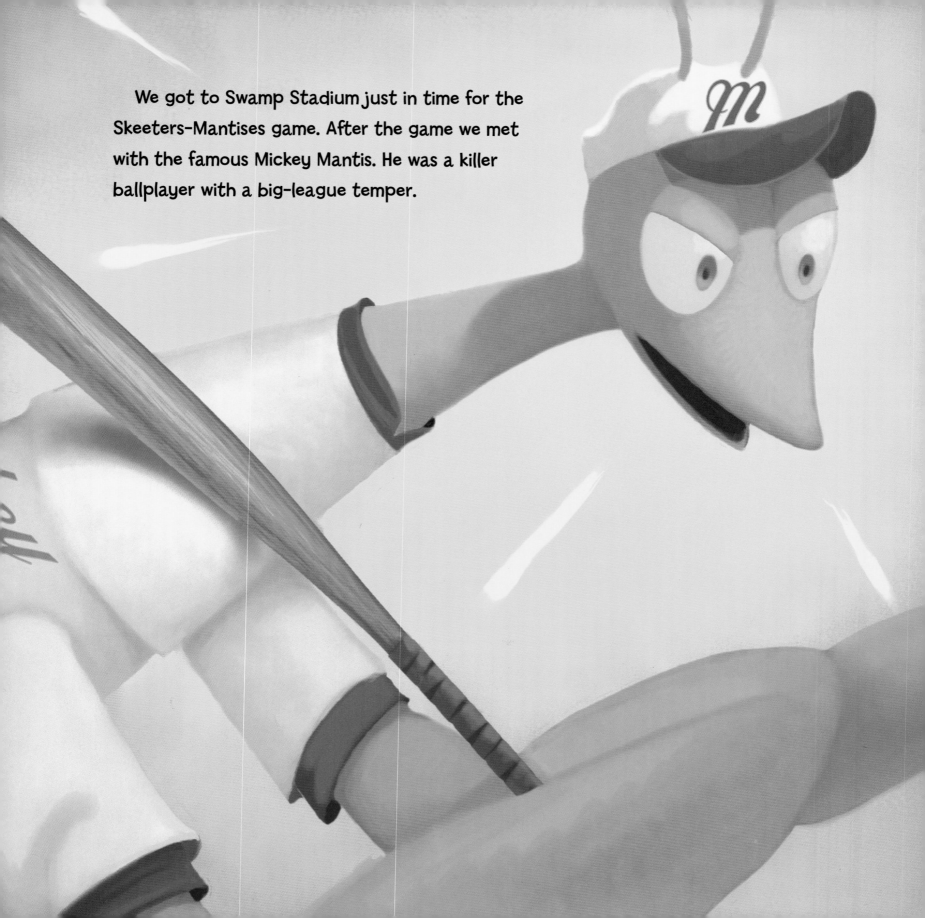

"Bugsy got what was coming to him, detective. A good hitter could hit with any bat!" the mantis hissed. "He was Madame Damselfly's little pet. That's why he won the contest. Everyone knows I was the best hitter in the orphanage. I should have won that bat.

"Next time you see Bugsy, tell him better luck next year. The Mantises are going all the way."

I couldn't wait to get out of there. The buzz around the league was that Mickey got the Mantis coach fired last season. Then he ate him.

In the Skeeters dugout was Zito's distant cousin Derek Skeeter. Everyone around the league liked Skeeter. They all knew he wanted his name on a bat someday. He was close to breaking Lou Earwig's record for the most hits by a bug leaguer. Skeeter had also been Bugsy's best friend at the orphanage. He was working on a scrapbook for him when we showed up. Pictures of Bugsy were all over the bench.

"I'm going to give it to him after the season," Skeeter said with a grin.

"I hope it has a happy ending," said Xerces.

"You got a lot of pictures of his lucky bat in there?" I asked.

Skeeter flinched. "Bugsy is the best player in the league, bat or no bat," he said. "We all have superstitions. Bugsy's got his bat. I have a pair of lucky socks. Big Hoppi has a thing about seven."

"You don't say," I muttered.

"If you ask me, Bugsy doesn't need his stinking bat back," Skeeter continued. "He needs to believe in himself first."

Li'l Slugger Wins "Lou Earwig" Autographed Bat

Li'l Larva Orphanage Wins Little League Title
Bugsy Goldwing MVP

Goldwing Leads Motham High School to Championship

Goldwing Signs with Stinkbugs

Rookie Goldwing Helps Stinkbugs Win First Game In Six Years

We said goodbye and headed home for the next night's game. The word was out all over Motham City that Bugsy's bat was missing—and we were no closer to finding it than when we started.

The next night the Crickets sang under
a full moon just before the game.

The crowd was buzzing with excitement.
Madame Damselfly sat in front of us, just
behind home plate, cheering for both Bugsy
and Hoppi. Whoever won tonight was going
to the play-offs.

The Leafhoppers got off to a quick 3-0 lead on a three-run homer by Hoppi in the top of the first.

Bugsy had no such luck. He struck out on his first at-bat, and slumped back to the dugout to a chorus of boos.

The score held through six and a half innings. During the seventh-inning stretch, the whole gang from Li'l Larva Orphanage, along with Mayor Buzzbee, showed up on the field. They called Madame Damselfly onto the field to present her with an award for her work at the orphanage.

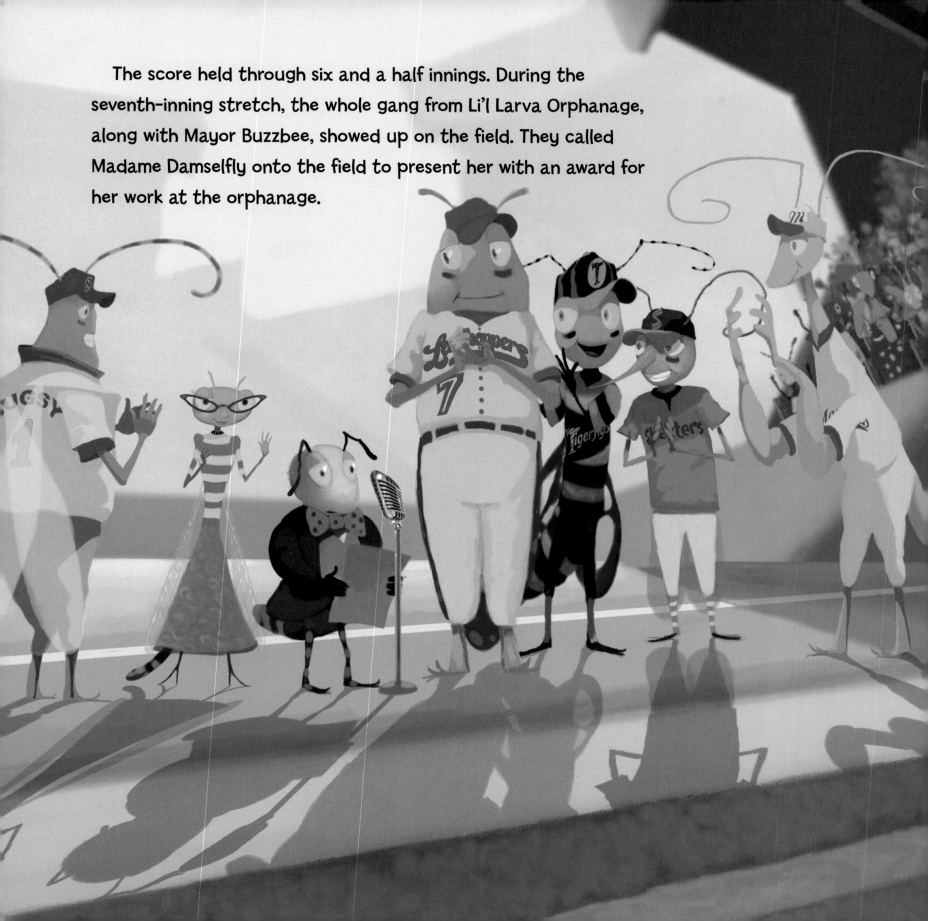

Pee Wee was supposed to give her the award. Problem was, Pee Wee was nowhere to be found. Things got quiet. Suddenly a security guard ran up from the Stinkbugs dugout.

"We need help! Pee Wee's hurt!"

We found Pee Wee out cold and facedown by the back exit.
He looked like he was in a hurry to leave the place.

When we looked closer, we realized why.

"Well, look at that," said Fly Cobb. "Sombody else wanted
that bat, too. You stink, Pee Wee!"

Bugsy looked stunned. "I thought Pee Wee was my friend."

"You don't need friends like that, Bugsy," said Skeeter.

"Are we done here, detective?" said Hoppi. "We have the seventh inning to finish."

"Yeah, let's get this game over with," said Mickey Mantis. "I'm getting hungry."

Bugsy stared at Pee Wee, still flat on the floor. "I'll need my bat, detective," he said softly. "Could you bring it up to the dugout after you're done?"

Then they all left for the field.

Xerces bent down to wake Pee Wee up.

"That's a nice new leg you've got there," I said. "Care to explain?"

Pee Wee blinked and looked confused.

"I—I don't know how that got there!" he cried. "I came down to the locker room to get the plaque for Madame Damselfly, and—oh, my head!"

"You're under arrest," said Zito. "Be careful what you say without a lawyer."

My antennae twitched. The hallway was littered with stuff, and it smelled sweet . . . too sweet.

Pee Wee rubbed the back of his head and moaned. My brain was buzzing. Then it hit me like a line drive.

"Wait a second," I said. "If you fell on your face, why are you rubbing the back of your head?"

I pulled off Pee Wee's hat. There was a lump the size of a baseball with the "Big Swat" trademark indented backward on it.

"Zito, Pee Wee wasn't stealing the bat. He was knocked out with it!" I said.

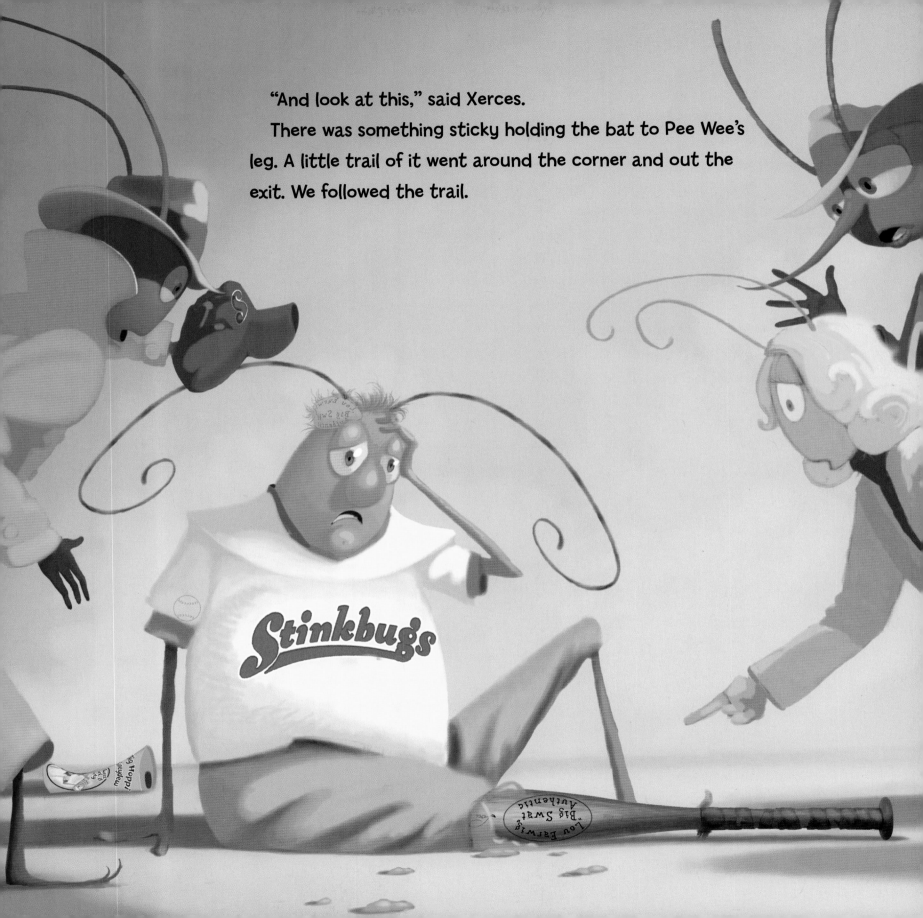

"And look at this," said Xerces.

There was something sticky holding the bat to Pee Wee's leg. A little trail of it went around the corner and out the exit. We followed the trail.

There he was, caught like a fly in a web—one of Hoppi's bodyguards, stuck in a puddle of Big Hoppi Honeydew. Sweet, thick, and very, very sticky.

As soon as he saw us, he started squealing.

"Don't hurt me!" he begged. "Hoppi made me do it. He made me bribe the roach and take the bat—all so he could get Bugsy out of the way and win his seventh MVP."

"And you couldn't live without your honeydew," I said.

"Hoppi has the best honeydew!" the ant sobbed. "I protect him; he feeds me. It's the leafhopper-ant code!"

"So why did you bring the bat back?" Xerces asked.

"Hoppi thought Bugsy's season was over. He wanted to get rid of the evidence," the little bug groaned.

"And set you up for the crime," I said.

"I'd do it again! I'd do anything for Hoppi!" whined the ant.

"Well, now you'll be serving time with him," I said.

As we snapped the cuffs on and headed back to the stands, we heard the crack of a bat—and a groan from the crowd.

Hoppi was on his way to third base when he spotted us with the little meat ant in handcuffs. He knew the jig was up, but he wanted one last chance to score. He picked up speed as he rounded third and headed home—straight into Bugsy.

The ball and Hoppi got there at the same time.

Hoppi came up seven aphids short of home plate. He was out in more ways than one.

The Leafhopper pitcher wasn't the same after Hoppi's arrest. He got two quick outs, but then he walked the bases full.

The crowd rumbled. Bugsy was up. He had his bat and his confidence back. But then Bugsy's shoulders slumped—and we saw the problem.

The bat was cracked.

Bugsy looked like his heart might break. He lumbered back to the dugout to get another bat. The crowd was silent—except for Madame Damselfly.

"Remember, Bugsy—it's not the size of the bat!" she yelled.

Bugsy looked at her, then squared up in the batter's box.

"It's the size of your heart," Bugsy whispered.

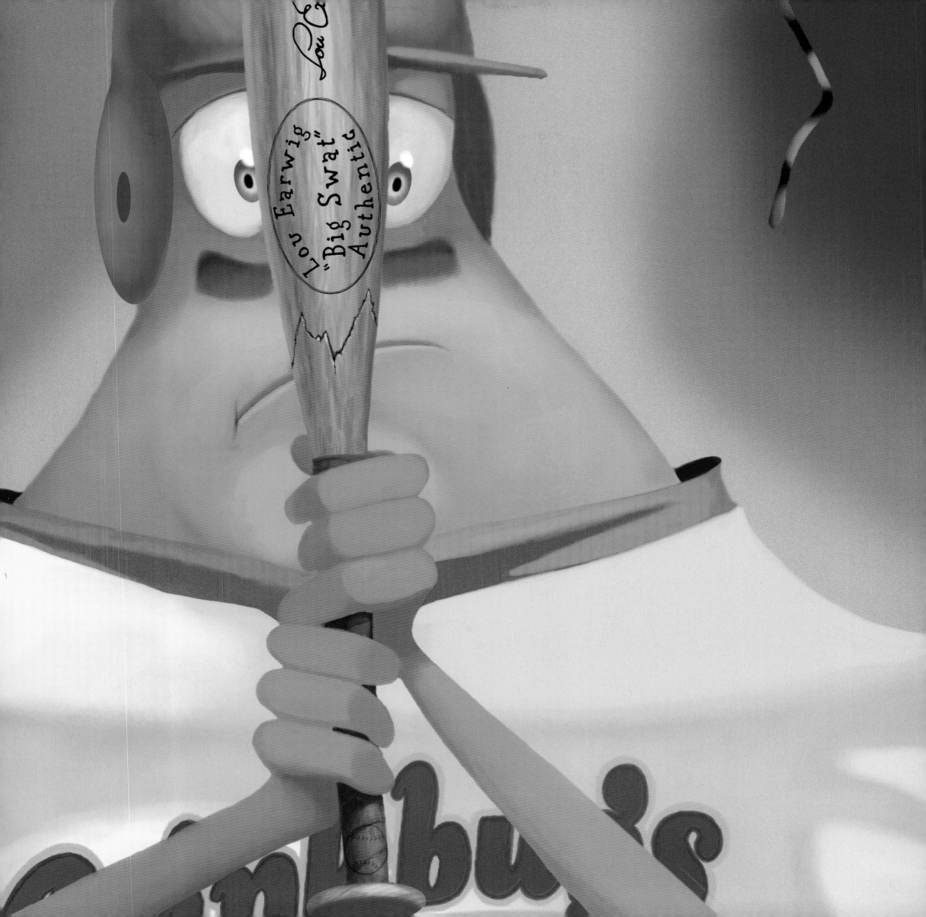

Some at the game that night said the ball Bugsy hit landed on the moon. Others said it was hit so hard that it's still going.

I know what really happened. That ball left Stinkbug Stadium and took Bugsy's superstition along with it. And after that?

It landed in my office.

To
Ace and Xerces,
Thanks for saving
my game.
Your friend,
Bugsy
Goldwing

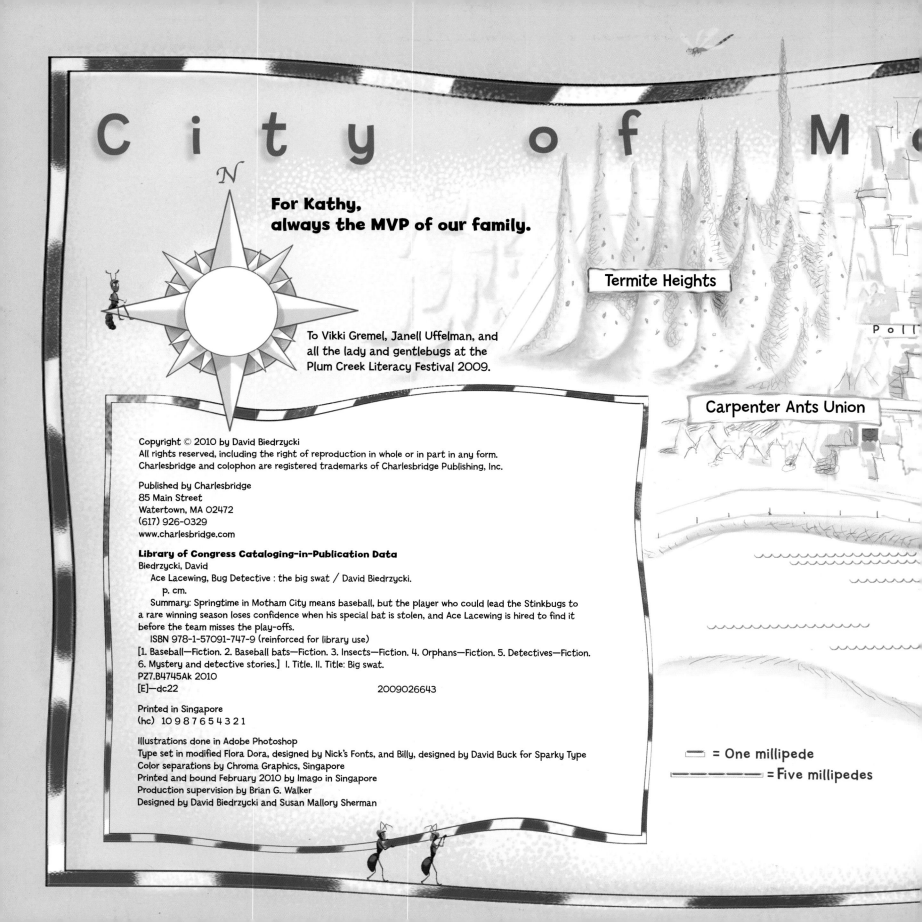

C i t y   o f   M

N

For Kathy,
always the MVP of our family.

Termite Heights

P o l l

To Vikki Gremel, Janell Uffelman, and
all the lady and gentlebugs at the
Plum Creek Literacy Festival 2009.

Carpenter Ants Union

Published by Charlesbridge
85 Main Street
Watertown, MA 02472
(617) 926-0329
www.charlesbridge.com

Library of Congress Cataloging-in-Publication Data
Biedrzycki, David
    Ace Lacewing, Bug Detective : the big swat / David Biedrzycki.
        p. cm.
    Summary: Springtime in Motham City means baseball, but the player who could lead the Stinkbugs to
a rare winning season loses confidence when his special bat is stolen, and Ace Lacewing is hired to find it
before the team misses the play-offs.
    ISBN 978-1-57091-747-9 (reinforced for library use)
[1. Baseball—Fiction. 2. Baseball bats—Fiction. 3. Insects—Fiction. 4. Orphans—Fiction. 5. Detectives—Fiction.
6. Mystery and detective stories.] I. Title. II. Title: Big swat.
PZ7.B4745Ak 2010
[E]—dc22   2009026643

Printed in Singapore
(hc) 10 9 8 7 6 5 4 3 2 1

Illustrations done in Adobe Photoshop
Type set in modified Flora Dora, designed by Nick's Fonts, and Billy, designed by David Buck for Sparky Type
Color separations by Chroma Graphics, Singapore
Printed and bound February 2010 by Imago in Singapore
Production supervision by Brian G. Walker
Designed by David Biedrzycki and Susan Mallory Sherman

⬜ = One millipede

⬜⬜⬜⬜⬜ = Five millipedes